A Pirate's Life for Gabby

Book 5 of **Revelry on the Estuary**

Text **Marlet Ashley**
Illustration **Kate Brown**

Publisher - Ashley Brown Books
www.ashleybrownbooks.com

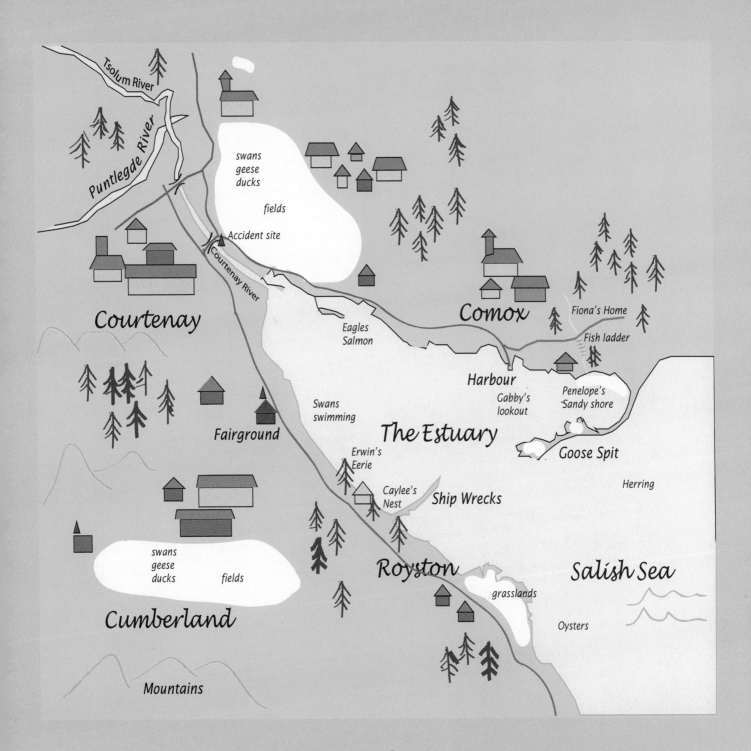

Tsolum River

Puntlegde River

swans
geese
ducks

fields

Accident site

Courtenay River

Courtenay

Eagles
Salmon

Comox

Fiona's Home

Fish ladder

Harbour

Gabby's
lookout

Penelope's
Sandy shore

Swans
swimming

The Estuary

Goose Spit

Fairground

Erwin's
Eerie

Caylee's
Nest

Ship Wrecks

Herring

swans
geese
ducks   fields

Royston

grasslands

Salish Sea

Cumberland

Oysters

Mountains

A Pirate's Life for Gabby

Gabby Gull was not always a pirate. In fact, he was an ordinary seagull living an ordinary life with all the other seagulls in the Comox Estuary until one fateful day in a particularly hot summer.

Gabby's life changed the day the mayor of Comox announced that for three evenings the town would show outdoor movies on a huge screen down at the harbour. The children were excited. When he announced that the movie would be about swashbuckling pirates, the children shouted for joy. They gathered up eye patches and play swords, put on high boots and brightly coloured headscarves.

On the days leading up to the movie, the children played pirate games on the sloping lawns before the harbour. The seagulls paid them little mind.

The children played pirate games on the lawns at Comox Harbour.

As the screen was set up, Gabby asked his flock of seagulls, "What are they planning?"

"Maybe it's a new kind of fishing net," answered his friend, Garnet.

"No," Gabby said, "they are raising it like a ship's sail not plunging it into the water"

The gulls watched as the townspeople gathered on the slopes of the parkland near the marina. When booths for selling refreshments and popcorn opened, the birds were beside themselves with glee.

Little black paper pirate hats, each decked with a skull and crossbones, held popcorn on which the gulls kept a close eye, especially Gabby.

The seaulls saw a big movie screen, and the popcorn boxes looked like pirate hats.

When darkness fell, the movie started, but Gabby stayed wide awake. His heart beat fast as he watched the wild pirates. Colourful, loud, sword-brandishing pirates! Pirates who called out pirate insults. Pirates who wore red bandanas on their heads and had huge gold rings in their ears.

Pirates who wore tall black boots with shining silver buckles. Pirates who climbed masts and shouted "Ahoy" from the ship's crow's nest. What action! What excitement! What a thrill! Gabby could hardly contain himself.

Gabby saw many wild and colourful pirates in the movie.

At first light, Gabby gathered his crew. "While ye slack-jawed, lazy-boned sea slugs be sleepin'," he cried, "I be makin' plans t'would stir the very bones 'o Davy Jones himself!" Gabby eyed his crew with only one eye. He kept the other closed.

When Garnet asked why he had his eye closed, Gabby answered, "Arrgh, ye short-sighted, squinty-eyed rapscallion, that's Cap'in Gabby to ye, ye empty-headed rollin' deck hand. It's so's the better t' spy wi' t' other eye."

"Aye, aye, Cap'in," said Garnet, for gulls are very smart and catch on quickly.

Gabby managed, not without difficulty, to get on his head one of the small black pirate hats used for holding popcorn. The crew of gulls looked at one another, but not one of them spoke. They were, to a bird, loyal to Gabby.

"Arrgh!" cried Gabby when he saw their questioning looks. "I be yer Cap'in, be I not, ya mutinous, lily sniffin beggars? An' I be wearin' a Cap'in's garb." That said, Gabby gave a sharp nod of his head, and the hat, which was quite large for him, slipped over one eye, the eye he had closed.

In unison, his crew said, "Aye, aye, Cap'in.'"

Gabby put a popcorn box on his head. It made him look like a pirate captain.

"Tonight," Gabby continued, "the lot o' ya weak-livered, kracken-headed flounders be stayin' awake ta view the adventures o' One-Eyed Jack, the most fearsome pirate that e're set sail upon the briny deep!" He explained how they could learn a thing or two by watching not only One-Eyed Jack but the pirate crew as well. He wanted them to see that no matter what Captain Jack asked his crew to do, they did it, no questions asked--Lift that barge. Tote that bale. Swab the decks. Walk the plank. Well, there would be no walking the plank, but Gabby liked to think that his crew was just as loyal as One-Eyed Jack's crew and would follow him into the fiercest battles or the roughest seas.

The next morning, the gulls were tired and squabbled with one another until Gabby could stand it no longer. "Hold yer tongues, ye mud-rakin', can-tankerous band o' thieves! We be havin' work to do today, work that be makin' us pirates true like."

Gabby's crew—Garnet, Gaston, Gregory, Gertrude, Gwen, and his nephew Gulliver--stopped their bickering and drew near Gabby to received their orders for the morning. They listened intently as Gabby explained that they were to become as rowdy a gang of pirates as One Eyed Jack and his band. The crew responded, "Aye, aye, Cap'in!"

But Garnet, as usual, had a question. "Cap'in Gabby," he began, "how be we true pirates without a ship an' a flag flyin' the Jolly Roger?" The others looked first to him and then to Gabby. They began to bob their heads in agreement. Gabby stopped to think for a moment.

We need a pirate ship," said Garnet Gull

"Ye be a bright one, ye be," he eventually said, with one eye covered by his hat and the other focused on Garnet, who was a little nervous and not at all sure if Gabby was pleased or angry. "If we be blood-thirsty buccaneers, to be sure we be needin' a ship, a right pirate ship!" Gabby said.
But where would they get one,
he and all the others wondered.
The pirate ship in the movie
had three masts, huge
billowing sails, and several
cannons lined up on either side.
Where would they find
such a vessel?

14

We need a pirate ship,"
said Garnet Gull

"Uncle Gabby," cried Gulliver, who was having a little trouble with pirate talk, "I know where we'll find a boat. It's not as big or as fancy as the one in the movie, but it is a boat, and it's abandoned. Follow me," he cried, and the crew took flight, following Gulliver to the shores of the estuary that faced the quiet lee side of Goose Spit.

Sure enough, stuck in the sand and sedge grass near where the Brooklyn Stream empties into the estuary was a little rowboat without oars. The gulls had seen this boat many, many times, but they never once thought of it as a pirate ship. They looked at the old wooden boat as if it were a frigate the likes of which the Comox Estuary had never before seen.

"Thar she be," crooned Gabby, who hopped aboard and stood at the bow of the little boat that faced the shore. Gabby ordered his crew to turn the ship about so they could head out to sea. The birds, however, had no idea how to go about moving such a heavy thing. Although the boat was small, it was not light, and it was stuck in the sand as well.

They grabbed hold of the sides of the little boat and heaved, but it did not budge. They grabbed hold of the bow and the stern and tried to rock it back and forth, but it did not move, not a millimetre.

"Arrgh! We be mutinous landlubbers for sure!" cried Gabby when he saw that the boat was stuck fast. Gabby noticed the high-water mark part way up the stern of the boat. If they came back when the tide was at its very highest, they could most certainly move the boat into deeper waters and turn it about, bow first.

The seagulls found a little rowboat
stuck in the sand, but the birds
couldn't get it out.

Silky, a little harbour seal,
joined Gabby's pirate crew.

Suddenly, a smooth and shiny head poked above the water. "What are you gulls up to?" said Silky Seal.

Gabby eyed the seal with his one eye. He had a bright idea. "We be pirates, me sweet silky sea maid," he said. "Arrrgh, an' we be needin some help-like when the high tide be comin in. What say ye? Would ye like to be part of our crew, me pretty?" Gabby could be very charming when he wanted to be.

"Why, I'd be honoured, Cap'in Gabby," said the little seal, eager for an adventure.

And so the gulls and seal agreed to meet when the tide was at its highest.

"Uncle Gabby," said Gulliver, "we should give our ship a name, something like the one in the movie—Neptune's Folly."

"That be Cap'in Gabby, me lad. Ye best be talkin pirate if ye be part o' my crew, Nephew." But Gulliver was right. They needed a name, one that would make them feared upon the high seas, or at least in the Comox Estuary.

"The Rowdy Rowboat?" offered Garnet, but Gabby looked at him so sternly with his piercing one eye, that Garnet shook his head and said, "No, no, that be not the one."

Gaston cried, " Pirates' Party," but that was not a name to instill fear.

"Fortune's Fancy," cried Gregory.

"Plenty O' Pearls," offered Gertrude.

Gwen shouted out, "Gulls' Revenge!"

And all the crew knew in their bones that this was the very name they needed. "GULLS' REVENGE!" they shouted all together.

The pirate seagulls called their ship Gulls' Revenge.

21

By six-thirty, the tide reached almost to the bow of the little boat. The gulls swarmed around, each one grabbing a part, some with their webbed feet and some with their powerful bills. Silky arrived and was able to work her way under the stern of the little rowboat.

"Heave!" cried Gabby, then "Ho!" as they flapped their wings and tugged with all of their might. Sure enough, as the boat was lifted little by little from the sand, the water rushed in and helped float the little craft. Before too long, the bow of the boat was no longer stuck.

With the help of the high tide, the newly-christened pirate ship made a neat turn in the water. Soon the tide began to recede taking the Gulls' Revenge and her crew out to deeper waters. The gulls cheered, Silky did a flip in the water, and Gabby moved to his place at the bow of the ship scouring the estuary for bounty.

The gulls and Silky worked very hard and finally got the little boat to float on the waves.

"Arrgh! We be right pirates, me hearties," exclaimed Gabby, and his crew answered back, "Arrgh!"

"Ahoy," cried Garnet. "Thar be a ship in me sights worth plunderin'!" He bobbed his head at a kayak paddled by one man.

"Avast, ye shark bait! We be plunderin' yer coffers!" shouted Gabby at the man who was very surprised to see a rowboat full of screaming seagulls followed by a harbour seal heading his way. He began to paddle faster, but he could not avoid the little boat as it drew alongside him. The gulls flapped their wings and plucked at his hair and hands. He had nothing to offer them since all was tucked away under the skirt of the kayak, but the birds swooped and rushed at him, and Silky bumped along the bottom of his vessel. The man pushed the little boat away with his paddle and quickly sped as far from them as he could. To his relief, the birds did not follow but remained with their boat that was drifting out to deeper waters.

"Arrgh!" Thar be no spoils tonight, ye half-perished privateers," said Gabby to his crew as they gathered in the gently rocking Gulls' Revenge.

The gulls saw a man in a kayak. "We're pirates," they called. "Give us your treasure." But the man paddled away.

By dawn, the little boat had been pulled by the tide and pushed by the current of the Courtenay River out into deep waters and a busy shipping channel.

Hard to starboard! Hard to starboard!" shouted a man as Gulls' Revenge headed straight for the side of his fishing boat. The gulls, however, did not yet understand the language of sailors. The right side of a ship is starboard and the left side is port. Mercifully, Silky poked her head up on the port side of the little pirate ship. She was a harbour seal, after all, and understood nautical terms. Silky pushed the Gull's Revenge toward starboard, avoiding a serious accident. Only a small mark remained on the vessel of the angry shouting man.

"Arrrgh," cried Captain Gabby. "Ye be one o' us, Silky, ye sharp-minded slip o' a sailor," and the motley crew filled the estuary with the sounds of their joy at once again being pirates in their pirate ship upon the deep blue sea.

26

The Gulls' Revenge bumped into a bigger boat. Silky tried to help, but the captain of the big boat was very angry.

27

Silky slipped below the ocean's surface. She came with an old bicycle wheel balanced on her nose and tossed it into Gulls' Revenge. "I be divin' for treasure," she said. All the birds cheered, and down she went again to see what she could bring up from the bottom.

"Ye be a treasure yourself, ye be," said Gabby to Silky as she tossed a small closed box into the little boat. A few tiny fish trapped in the box made a tasty snack for the gulls.

Up came the harbour seal again, this time with an old rusted can. Again and again Silky went to the bottom and brought up whatever she could find—a chain, an old tire, several boots, and a number of plates and cups—sunken treasure, to be sure. Before long, the little boat overflowed with riches Silky brought up from below. Soon it was clear that the little boat could hold no more. In fact, even before Silky started diving for treasure, the boat, which had been stuck on shore for as long as anyone could remember, was slowly filling with water.

Silky the seal dove to the bottom of the sea. She brought up a boot and a tire and many other treasures.

The gulls laughed and rolled in the treasure that sat in the Gulls' Revenge.

30

"We be plunderin' the sea today, me hearties," Gabby told his crew. "Thar be gold down below," he said, "gold enough ta cap yer teeth ten times over, ye sorry seadogs." He was repeating what Captain One-Eyed Jack said in the movie.

"Cap'in,'" asked Garnet, never one to be afraid of asking a question, "what be caps? And what we be needin' caps for if we no be havin' teeth?"

Gabby gave his first mate a cold stare with his one eye.

"Me thinks we be needin' food, Cap'in," offered Gaston.

"Aye, foooood," chimed in Gregory.

"We be havin' fish 'n chips, me thinks," said Gertrude.

"Or maybe we be feastin' on sumpin' fancy like goose liver paté!" Gwen said loudly in her gruff pirate voice.

"Har, har, har," they all joined in. "Goose liver paté! Har, har, har!" The crew rolled around in the plunder carried by the little boat, splitting their sides with laughter.

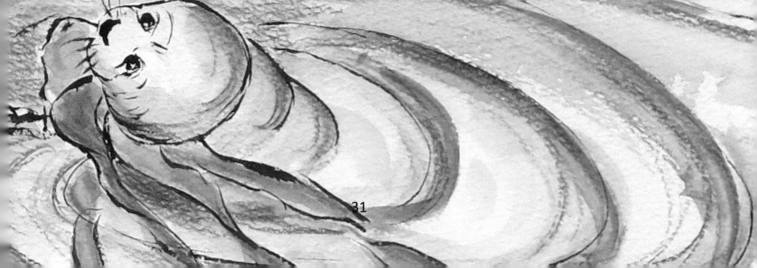

31

Captain Gabby looked cautiously at the water rising in Gulls' Revenge. "Avast, ye flea bitten sons 'o sea foam," cried Gabby. "Shut yer pie holes an' keep watch. The ship be near ta sinkin'," for the little boat was riding low on the waves.

"Uncle Gabby," cried Gulliver. "I don't think we…"

"Be ye afeard, nephew Gulliver?" Gabby asked in a slow and menacing voice. "Be ye about ta jump ship or mutiny, ye lily-livered shark bait?"

"No, Uncle Gabby!" Gulliver sputtered. "No, no. I just thought we might throw some of this stuff overboard to lighten the boat."

"Ye have learnin', ye young scallywag, but yer books be not teachin' ya bravery in the face o' danger, be they," scolded Gabby. He turned from his nephew and looked back out to sea. Although he expected his crew to be brave, Gabby felt his legs shaking, for Gulls' Revenge was most certainly sinking, and even with a crew of seven, eight counting Silky the harbour seal, they were no match for the great wide and deep ocean.

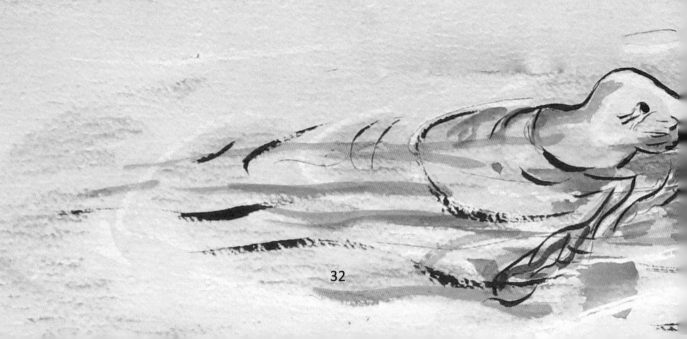

Too much treasure in the little boat made it sink.

Garnet, Gaston, Gregory, Gertrude, Gwen, and Gulliver all began to cry at once, "Abandon ship, abandon ship!" but Gabby held firm to the bow. Silky swam beneath to try to hold the boat afloat, but it was no use. So much treasure from the deep along with the rising water proved too much for her to bear.

The stern went down first, and all the birds but Gabby flew away. Gabby stayed on the bow of Gulls' Revenge until he was resting on the ocean waves. He stayed floating on the spot where his ship went down until near nightfall. He was angry at his crew for leaving, and he was sad at losing his one and only pirate ship. Silky tried to cheer him up by staying close, but Gabby was silent in the face of such disappointment.

Gabby floated on the spot where his boat sank, and he was very sad.

Gabby paid Silky little mind. He remained silent until he heard another pirate movie starting in the harbour. All of a sudden, Gabby flew back over the Comox Estuary, searching for the crew that had abandoned ship.

Gabby flew back to the harbour to see
the movie and find his friends.

"Arrrgh, ye chicken-livered motley crew o' mine. Where be ye? Ye be walkin' the plank 'afore long if ye be thinkin' this be the end o' our pirate ways. We be losin' our ship, but we be scowerin' the skies, floatin' on the wind lookin' for bounty from the witless landlubbers!"

And with that, he swooped down and grabbed a bill full of popcorn from an unsuspecting teenager then joined his crew atop the big willow tree in the park to watch another swashbuckling pirate movie.

Gabby shouted, "We be pirates, yet!"
He grabbed a bill full of popcorn from a boy.

From that day to this, Gabby and his crew have been pirates right and true, stealing and marauding for food and trinkets wherever they could, but they never went to sea in a boat again, preferring to look for treasures close to home and to meet up with Silky who gathered what plunder she could from the deep.

But every day, humans came along and picked up Silky's treasures, collecting the tires and inner tubes, boots and buckets, bottles and boxes in big green garbage bags. And every day, Gabby and his crew plotted their revenge on the witless thieving landlubbers—"Arrrrgh!"

**Gabby and his crew
became pirates on land.
Silky brought them treasures
from the ocean bottom, but
people kept cleaning it all up. "Arrgh!"**

Revelry on the Estuary Series

Book 1   The Interlopers

When an accident happens on the Fifth Street Bridge, the birds of the estuary are alarmed by what has fallen into the water. It takes an act of courage and some quick thinking to save the birds from the interlopers.

ISBN-10: 1492111163 ISBN-13: 978-1492111160

Book 2   Trumpeters' Tribulations

Sampson, a young swan is troubled by insults from the ducks and gulls, but a wise old swan tells him of days gone by and how the trumpeters have survived worse things than a few unkind words.

ISBN-10: 1492111791 ISBN-13: 978-1492111795

Book 3   Penelope Piper's Great Adventure

Life as a sandpiper has become very boring for Penelope, so she seeks a new adventure with her new-found friend, Fiona frog. She has no idea what is in store for her as she travels far from the seashore.

ISBN-10: 1482338602 ISBN-13: 978-1482338607

Book 4   Henri Sings the Blues

A lonely blue heron who, with the help of a very unlikely source, learns the secret of making new friends and is happily surprised by friends he has.

ISBN-10: 1495470407 ISBN-13: 978-1495470400

Book 5   A Pirate's Life for Gabby

Gabby was not always a pirate. After watching a swashbuckling pirate movie, he got some bright ideas about how he and his friends could rule the briny deep.

ISBN-10: 978 1511825324 ISBN-13: 9871511825320

Available from local book stores and on-line from
amazon.com Marlet Ashley

Marlet Ashley, the author, is a long-time educator with an M.A. in English Literature and Creative Writing. She taught creative writing at the University of Windsor and was an instructor of literature and composition at Kwantlen Polytechnic University. Along with the children's books series *Revelry on the Estuary—The Interlopers, Trumpeters' Tribulations, Penelope Piper's Great Adventure,* and *Henri Sings the Blues*—as well as a children's Christmas book—*Must Be Christmas*—her short stories and poetry have been included in a variety of literary publications. She is the author of the Canadian edition of *Literature and the Writing Process,* Pearson Prentice Hall, Toronto. Marlet is an executive member of the Comox Valley Writers Association and leads a fiction writing group. A finalist for the 2012 John Kenneth Galbraith Literary Award, Marlet lives in Comox, BC.

Kate Brown, the illustrator, studied Art and Design in London, UK, and developed a career as an interior designer, product designer, and clothing designer. Kate has been involved in designing museums in which exhibited artefacts are seemingly brought to life to tell stories that enthral and capture the interest of visitors. She has illustrated the children's books series *Revelry on the Estuary—The Interlopers, Trumpeters' Tribulations, Penelope Piper's Great Adventure and Henri Sings the Blues*—as well as a children's Christmas book—*Must Be Christmas.* To accompany the series, Kate has produced a number of prints and original paintings as well as ceramic ware depicting the books' characters. Kate is president and founding member of the Art Group of the Comox Valley, an organization that encourages artists and also supports local charities through art. Kate lives in Courtenay, BC on the Courtenay Estuary.

visit us again at

Ashley Brown Books

www.ashleybrownbooks.com